DJANGO

story by JOHN CECH

pictures by SHARON McGINLEY-NALLY

FOUR WINDS PRESS ❋ New York

MAXWELL MACMILLAN CANADA   Toronto
MAXWELL MACMILLAN INTERNATIONAL   New York   Oxford   Singapore   Sydney

I wish to gratefully thank the Florida Department of State's Division
of Cultural Affairs for its support, through an Individual Artist Fellowship,
which helped me to complete this book. —J.C.

Special thanks to Lydia Elliott, Forest Harrington, Piera Snyder,
and the Peterman family, and an extra special thanks to "the King."
—S.M.-N.

Text copyright © 1994 by John Cech
Illustrations copyright © 1994 by Sharon McGinley-Nally

Four Winds Press
Macmillan Publishing Company
866 Third Avenue
New York, NY 10022

Maxwell Macmillan Canada, Inc.
1200 Eglinton Avenue East
Suite 200
Don Mills, Ontario M3C 3N1

Macmillan Publishing Company is part of the
Maxwell Communication Group of Companies.
First edition
Printed in Hong Kong by South China Printing Company (1988) Ltd.
on chlorine-free, acid-free paper
10 9 8 7 6 5 4 3 2 1
The text of this book is set in Novarese Medium.
The illustrations in this book were primarily painted with
Rotring Artists Colors, a liquid watercolor that produces very vivid colors.
In order to give readers a feel for the woods surrounding Django's home,
the artist sponged two to three layers of an all-natural beverage containing malt,
chicory, rye, figs, and beet roots onto her watercolor paper.
Book design by Christy Hale
Library of Congress Cataloging-in-Publication Data
Cech, John.
Django / story by John Cech ; pictures by Sharon McGinley-Nally.—
1st ed.
p.   cm.
Summary: In this retelling of a Floridian legend,
a boy learns to fiddle and later uses his music to save the forest animals
from the floods caused by a hurricane.
ISBN 0-02-765705-1
[1. Folklore—Florida. 2. Folklore—United States.] I. McGinley-Nally, Sharon, ill. II. Title.
PZ8.1.C29Dj   1994
398.21—dc20
[E]   93-46782

DJANGO lived way back in the woods with his mother and father and his Grandma Thelma. Their house was made of cypress boards with chinks between them wide enough to let a moonbeam squeeze through, strong enough to hold back wind and rain.

Django loved to listen to all sorts of sounds—especially the ones animals make, like the way a frog *kereeck-kereecks* in the pond and a dog *ahwooooos* at a train whistle. He loved the way your toes sing *kush, kush, kush* when you walk in mud in your bare feet. He loved to make up his own sounds, too. That's how he got his name. It was his first sound when he was a baby. He mixed together "da" with "jangle," added "banjo" for good luck, and out came "*Django, Django, Django.*"

Most of all Django loved to fiddle. For years his grandfather's fiddle had been tucked away at the bottom of the family trunk, snug between the holiday quilts. Django's father took it out one day and put it in the boy's hands.

"I never could get very far with it," his father said as he showed Django how to tune the strings.

Django did the rest. One day he was screeching around the yard, and the next he was playing a sweet melody. From the time the chickens got up in the morning until the cows went to sleep at night, Django's fingers danced over the strings of his grandfather's fiddle.

Soon Django was making up his own music. He strung all the bird songs he'd ever heard into one song. He was sitting on the fence playing the fiddle, and the birds began to settle everywhere. They stayed for the song, but then they stayed and helped themselves to the seeds they found in the garden. Django's father was mad. He had to plant the garden all over again, and he almost took the fiddle away.

But Django's mother said, "We can't blame Django because his music makes the birds want to stop and listen."

Django promised not to play bird songs anywhere near the garden anymore, and he kept his word. He knew the woods like his own backyard, and so he went there to try out any songs he thought the birds or animals might like. He made up one that had raccoons and possums for miles around tapping their tails and slapping their paws.

"It's a good thing we're a mile away from Daddy's garden," Django told his audience as the last notes of his song drifted off between the trees. "You sure would be a lot of company for dinner!"

But the more Django played in the woods, the more he forgot his chores around the house. Soon his mother was vexed because Django didn't fill the wood bin or gather the eggs or fetch the water or do any of the dozen things that he was supposed to do. "Seems to me that fiddle belongs back in the trunk," she said to Grandma Thelma.

"Don't be too angry with the boy," Grandma Thelma said as she rocked. "He's just following his heart's desire, and it'll break his heart to lose that fiddle. Leave him be for a little longer. He'll come around—you'll see."

One day Django went into the woods with Grandma Thelma to help her pick blackberries. When they stopped for a rest, Django played a new song full of deep bass notes. It wasn't long before they heard loud rustling in the bushes behind them.

Now, Grandma Thelma knew her way around the woods, too, and she could tell if a leaf was made to dance by a raindrop falling or a dragonfly springing, and she didn't like the weight of some of those rustlings. They had a bear in them, maybe two.

"Just keep playing," she whispered, "and we'll ease around and head for home."

"It's all right, Grandma," Django whispered back. "They won't bother us. I've seen them before. It's a mama bear and her cub."

Grandma Thelma was in no mood to stop and visit, so they hurried back home through the woods. But the bears followed them into the pasture where the horses were grazing and right up to the porch steps. The horses bolted at the first whiff of the bears, and it took Django and his father a whole afternoon to find them and coax them back to their meadow.

That did it.

The fiddle went back to its silent place in the trunk.

After that the wood bin was full, the eggs were gathered, and the dishes were dried and stacked nice and neat on the shelves. The garden was hoed and watered, and the porch was swept clean. But something was missing. The chickens knew it. They laid fewer eggs. The cows knew it. They gave less milk. The birds stopped singing outside the house, and Django just wasn't himself during those hot, still, quiet days.

Then one day the sky turned gray, then black, then purple-black. The wind whipped the tops of the trees into tangles, and it drove the rain sideways at the house, trying to push it between the cypress boards.

Django and Grandma Thelma and Django's mother and father all sat close together in the kitchen, waiting for the storm to pass. But it grew even stronger, and soon the storm was trying to tear the shingles off the roof, and soon it was howling and running into trees and knocking them over on its way to who knows where.

"The woods will be flooding," Django's father said, rubbing his chin with worry. "It's a good thing we're on high ground. But those animals out in the woods are going to be in a terrible fix—even the ones that can swim."

"We need to help them!" Django cried.

"Now, Django, there's nothing we can do for those poor creatures," his mother told him gently.

"Can I play my fiddle for them?" Django asked. "They know my songs, and maybe a few of them will hear and follow the sounds up here."

"They won't hear a thing in this storm, son," his father said. "But sure you can play. We could all use some music right now."

So the fiddle was found again and tuned, and Django played while the storm howled around the house. By nightfall Django ran out of the songs he knew and found himself climbing the notes of a melody he had never played before.

The song had ripples in it that sounded like water rushing down a stream, splashing against smooth stones, and then lingering at a bend among some red and yellow leaves.

The melody had a sadness in it for all the animals caught in the storm and for all the broken, fallen trees. Django's song had the mist of morning in it, when the first whippoorwill sings and the world wakes up again.

Django played the song softly through the night and into the morning, until Grandma Thelma and his parents stirred themselves awake and his father put the kettle on. The wind and rain had stopped, the lightning and thunder had quit shaking the house. But now other sounds moved above and all around them. The roof was sighing and settling, and outside the porch was purring.

"Now, whatever can that be?" Grandma Thelma asked as she began to open the shutters.

"Well . . . well . . . well," she said, in the way that meant she was truly surprised. "Looks like we've got company."

On every spot above the reach of the rising water, birds and animals were waiting out the storm, listening to Django's best song ever. And as they listened, slowly, slowly, a light wind pulled the clouds apart like tufts of cotton and let the sun shine through.

Paris Miracle was their nearest neighbor, from the next farm along the spring, and he came to see if Django and his family were all right. There was so much water in the woods and the fields that he had to row over in his boat. And he couldn't get near the house because of all the animals that were perched on it and resting all around. Later he told everyone, "It was just like Noah's ark!"

After that storm the fiddle never went back into the trunk again. Django managed to get his chores done, mostly, except he might be a little late if he was in the middle of a new tune. The birds left the garden alone, pretty much, and that summer the horses and cows even got used to the bear and her cub dropping by for an evening concert.

Music travels fast in the woods, and Django's music traveled everywhere. People came from miles away to sit on the porch and listen to him fiddle, and soon they were taking Django all over to play for their weddings and socials, their wingdings and holiday dances.

Why, Django was even invited to Washington to play for the president's birthday, and he made up a new bird song for the occasion that filled the trees around the White House with cardinals and doves and bluebirds.

ut there was one song Django always saved for the long walks he took back in the woods, the song he found on the night of the storm, the song that was like a dream—of feathers and warm fur, of shadows swaying high up in the branches of the trees.

All this happened years and years ago. But folks around here say that on quiet, moonlit evenings, if you go deep into the heart of the woods, you can still hear Django playing his song. And the animals . . . well, the animals are . . . dancing.

A NOTE ON THE STORY

The idea for *Django* is about fifteen years old. It began when I first heard the tales about one of northern Florida's legendary fiddlers, Cush Holston. Cousin Thelma Boltin, who was, in her lifetime, an encyclopedia of Florida folklore, had told me how Cush played with such "ethereal beauty" that the animals would appear from the woods around his house near Cedar Key, Florida, to sit and listen to his music. Later, I heard Florida's two extraordinary troubadours, the late Gamble Rogers and Will McLean, celebrate Cush in their songs and stories. Will told another remarkable tale about how Cush, when he knew the end of his life was near, simply put his fiddle in a sack and vanished into the woods, never to be seen again. These stories started my imaginings of the childhood of a magical fiddler. *Django* is the result of that process and is my homage to the memory of the gentle, generous spirits of Thelma, Will, and Gamble, who brought a grace to this life through the poetry of their songs and stories, and who are all telling tales and making music together somewhere way back in the woods of Florida.

—J.C.

A NOTE ON DJANGO'S HOUSE

The high roof and large porch of Django's house were inspired, in part, by the home of Marjorie Kinnan Rawlings in Cross Creek, Florida. The Rawlings Homestead, where the author wrote her famous book *The Yearling* (1938), is in the National Register of Historic Sites and is preserved by the Florida Department of Natural Resources Division of Recreation and Parks in much the same way that Mrs. Rawlings left it. The house and grounds welcome visitors, and the kettle is usually simmering on the "classic" stove in the kitchen.

—S.M.-N.